# Aron Goes to the White House Science Fair

## Written By Nahjee Grant
## Illustrated By Justine Babcock

This book is dedicated to the
memory of Donovan Bryant

Printed in the United States of America

Published by: Aces Klick Books

For more information please visit:

www.nahjeegrant.com

In 1753, Benjamin Banneker created the first clock ever made in the United States by carving each piece by hand.

On September 12, 1992, Dr. Mae Jemison was the first woman of color to blast off into space aboard shuttle STS−47 Endeavor.

In 1966, Marie Brown wanted to feel
more safe at home. She had the idea
for a camera to show images on a
monitor in her home. Her invention
led to the beginning of the modern
home security system.

Known to many as the "King of Pop"
Michael Jackson was the greatest
entertainer in the world. He also
created anti-gravity shoes that gave
him the illusion of leaning forward,
first shown in 1987.

Kanye West is widely considered one of the most influential music artists and reshaped Hip—Hop since his first album, College Dropout, in 2004. His passion for fashion led him to establish a new design company, Donda, named after his mother.

Elon Musk is a man who wears many hats. With a passion for science, business, and technology, Elon is the founder of the payment system Paypal as well as the science and technology companies SpaceX and Tesla.

Nahjee Grant is a published children's book author aimed to teach the importance of children to pursue their passion. He is also the founder of home-to-school communications company Let's Collab.

SOURCES & FURTHER INFORMATION

Websites:

Kanye West (2015). In Bio.com. Retrieved from
http://www.biography.com/people/kanye-west-362922

Kanye West (2015). In Complex. Retrieved from
http://www.complex.com/style/2014/11/
how-kanye-wests-creative-company-donda-is-making-its-own-brand-of-cool

Elon Musk. (2015). In Encyclopædia Britannica. Retrieved from
eg0http://www.britannica.com/EBchecked/topic/1676437/Elon-Musk

Michael Jackson. (2015) In Smithsonian. Retrieved from
http://www.smithsonianmag.com/arts-culture/
michael-jackson-singer-songwriter-american-inventor-180950165/?no-ist

Benjamin Banneker. (2015) In Bnl.gov. Retrieved from
http://www.bnl.gov/bera/activities/globe/banneker.htm

Mae Jemison. (2015) In Scholastic. Retrieved from
http://teacher.scholastic.com/space/mae_jemison/

Marie Brown. (2015). In About.com. Retrieved from
http://inventors.about.com/library/inventors/blhomesecurity.htm

Nahjee Grant. (2015). In Delco Times. Retrieved from
http://www.delcotimes.com/social-affairs/20150508/
website-aims-to-help-bring-teachersparents-together